A Watermelon in the Sukkah

Sylvia A. Rouss and Shannan Rouss

illustrated by Ann Iosa

KAR-BEN
PUBLISHING

To Hayden, Derek, and Leo,
with Love—Mimi and Aunt Shannan

In loving memory of my parents
Helen and Frederick Wisneski;
with appreciation for their lifelong
encouragement and support— Ann Iosa

Text copyright © 2013 by Sylvia A. Rouss and Shannan Rouss
Illustrations copyright © 2013 Lerner Publishing Group, Inc.

KAR-BEN PUBLISHING, INC.
A division of Lerner Publishing Group, Inc.
241 First Avenue North
Minneapolis, MN 55401 U.S.A.
1-800-4-Karben

Website address: www.karben.com

Library of Congress Cataloging-in-Publication Data

Rouss, Sylvia A.
    A watermelon in the sukkah / by Sylvia A. Rouss and Shannan Rouss ; illustrated by
Ann Iosa.
      pages   cm
    Summary: A class of preschool students wonders how to hang a watermelon in the
sukkah.
    ISBN 978–0–7613–8118–1 (lib. bdg. : alk. paper)
    ISBN 978–1–4677–1642–0 (eBook)
    [1. Sukkah—Fiction. 2. Fruit—Fiction. 3. Schools—Fiction.] I. Rouss, Shannan. II. Iosa,
Ann, illustrator. III. Title.
PZ7.R7622Wat 2013
[E]—dc23   2012028984

Manufactured in the United States of America
1 – PC – 7/15/13

Miss Sharon was closing the door to the classroom, as Michael rushed in, rolling a big green watermelon. "Wait for me!" he called.

It was the day the children were bringing their favorite fruits to hang in the school sukkah. Sam brought an apple, Rachel came in with a pear, David was carrying an orange, and Julie took a tangerine out of her backpack. There were also grapes, pomegranates, and bananas on the table.

"You are so silly, Michael," Rachel giggled. "You can't hang a watermelon in a sukkah."

"But watermelon is my favorite fruit," Michael protested.

Miss Sharon smiled. "Let's go out to the sukkah," she said, "and maybe we can figure out a way to help Michael hang his watermelon."

The children followed her to the sukkah. It had wood beams on all four sides, branches for a roof, and fabric for the walls It felt like you were outside even when you were inside.

Miss Sharon helped the children tie strings around their fruits.
Then they took turns hanging them. Soon apples, oranges,
bananas, and grapes were dangling from the sukkah branches.
Michael sat patiently with his watermelon cradled in his lap.

"Who has an idea for how we can hang Michael's favorite fruit?" Miss Sharon asked.

"Maybe if we use a lot of string and wrap it around the watermelon, we can hang it," said Julie.

"Let's try," Miss Sharon said. But each time they lifted the watermelon, the string slipped off.

"How about hanging the watermelon with lots of tape?" suggested Sam.

"Let's try," Miss Sharon said.

But each time they lifted the watermelon, the tape ripped.

David shouted, "Maybe we can stretch rubber bands around the watermelon and hang it!"

"Let's try," Miss Sharon said. But each time they lifted the watermelon, the rubber bands snapped.

"Nothing's going to work," Rachel said. "You'll have to hold it up in the air, Michael."

Michael stood in the middle of the sukkah and lifted his watermelon up toward the branches.

two seconds,

He held it for one second,

three seconds.

But then his arms got tired. He set the watermelon down and sighed. "Maybe my favorite fruit can't hang in the sukkah after all."

Back in the classroom, Miss Sharon consoled him. "Michael, maybe you should bring your second favorite fruit tomorrow."

Michael looked down at his watermelon. "I don't think so," he said sadly.

"Now that we're done decorating, can we play on the swings?" Julie whispered to Miss Sharon. She looked hopefully at the playground nearby.

Michael looked outside, too. "Wait a second!" he called. "I have an idea!"

The other children were surprised, but excited.

"Tell us," they begged.

"Miss Sharon," Michael asked, "is there any leftover cloth from the sukkah walls?"

"I think so," Miss Sharon said. She searched through her big bag of sukkah supplies.

"Here," she said, pulling out a square of fabric and handing it to Michael.

Michael asked David, Sam, Rachel, and Julie to each hold a corner of the cloth. Then he gently placed the watermelon in the center.

"It's a watermelon swing!" he said.

Miss Sharon helped Michael and the other children attach hooks to each corner of the cloth. Then they went outside and hung it in the sukkah.

When they were finished, they all looked up.

"It's wonderful!" exclaimed David.

"I love it!" cried Rachel.

"It's beautiful!" Julie nodded.

"And tomorrow," Michael shouted, "I'm going to bring my second favorite fruit!"

"What is that?" Miss Sharon asked.

"A pumpkin!"

About Sukkot

The Jewish holiday of Sukkot recalls the temporary huts the Jewish people built and lived in as they wandered in the desert after the biblical Exodus from Egypt. This fall holiday also celebrates the harvest. Jewish families around the world build and decorate sukkot outside their homes and synagogues, and often eat their meals there.

About the Authors
Sylvia A. Rouss is the award-winning author of the popular "Sammy Spider" series and many other children's books. Also an early childhood educator, the children in her classroom have been her inspiration. This is her second collaboration with her daughter **Shannan Rouss**, author of *Easy for You* (Simon & Schuster).

About the Illustrator
Ann Iosa is a graduate of Paier School of Art where she studied illustration and design. Her artwork reflects her love of nature, children and animals. She works primarily in watercolor and acrylics but also in pen and ink and digitally. She lives in Connecticut in the middle of the woods surrounded by wildlife, with her husband and two grown children.